Ultimate Sticker Collection

Disney · PIXAR
FINDING DORY

HOW TO USE THIS BOOK

Read the captions, then find the sticker that best fits the space. (Hint: check the sticker labels for clues!)

•

Don't forget that your stickers can be stuck down and peeled off again.

•

There are lots of fantastic extra stickers too!

 DK | Penguin Random House

Written by Glenn Dakin
Edited by Lisa Stock
Designed by Chris Gould
Editorial assistance by Lauren Nesworthy
Additional design by Stefan Georgiou, Anna Formanek, Anna Pond, and Anne Sharples
Jacket designed by Chris Gould

First American Edition, 2016
Published in the United States by DK Publishing
345 Hudson Street, New York, New York 10014

Page design copyright © 2016 Dorling Kindersley Limited
DK, a Division of Penguin Random House LLC
16 17 18 19 20 10 9 8 7 6 5 4 3 2
002–260178–May/2016

Published in Great Britain by Dorling Kindersley Limited.

A catalog record for this book is available from the Library of Congress.
ISBN: 978-1-4654-4979-5

DK books are available at special discounts when purchased in bulk for sales promotions, premiums, fund-raising, or educational use. For details, contact: DK Publishing Special Markets, 345 Hudson Street, New York, New York 10014
SpecialSales@dk.com

Printed and bound in China

A WORLD OF IDEAS:
SEE ALL THERE IS TO KNOW

www.dk.com
www.disney.com

REEF LIFE

This colorful coral reef is in fact a vibrant undersea city, teeming with life. It has its own schools, playgrounds, and busy highways. Of course, to those at the top of the food chain, it's also a big snack bar!

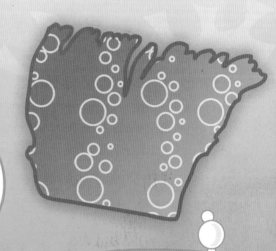

Sea View
With ocean views to be proud of, this family-size anemone is the perfect home for a clownfish couple.

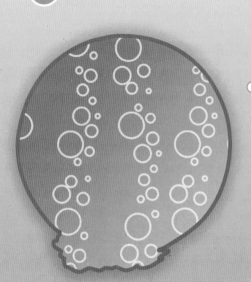

Best of Fronds
A curtain of anemone fronds is perfect for peeping through to see if the coast is clear. Clownfish don't feel their nasty stings.

Handsome Hutch
This fancy angelfish is one of the most beautiful in the ocean. Stripes and spots never go out of fashion.

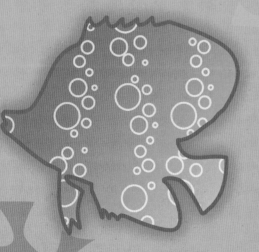

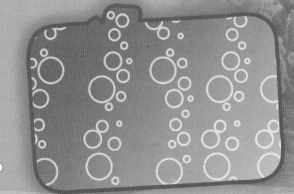

Coral Corner
On the reef, coral comes in every shape and size. It's great for hiding in or just hanging out and enjoying the view.

THE STORY OF DORY

On a pretty coral reef, surrounded by soft sea grass, lives a family of Regal Tangs. Although baby Dory has a memory problem, these affectionate fish somehow know that whatever happens, they will never truly forget each other.

Mama Dory
A kind and patient mother, Jenny tries to teach her daughter games and songs that will help her improve her memory.

Baby Dory
As a little fish, Dory often forgets the game she's playing and starts playing in the sand—which she loves because it's squishy!

Lost!
After being separated from her mom and dad, Dory spends her childhood traveling the sea to find them again.

Learning to Seek
Dory likes hide and seek. Soon all that practice will come in useful when she needs to find her parents.

Meeting Marlin
Dory and Marlin soon become good friends, although it does take Dory a little while to win round a certain Mr. Grumpy Gills!

Dory's Dad
This fond father calls Dory his little kelpcake. He helps her lay down a line of shells so she can find her way home.

A New Life
Dory finds a family—although it's not the one she started out with! Marlin and Nemo give her a new home.

Remembering
The past may be a bit foggy for Dory, but sometimes she has flashbacks and sees the clearest pictures of the people she loves.

FATHER AND SON

Nemo is a cute clownfish with a sense of adventure. Marlin is a fussy father, who doesn't want his son to take any chances. This pair have a knack of getting into adventures and making the most unexpected friends.

Sole Survivor
Marlin is extra protective of his son. Nemo is the only one of his babies to survive a terrible barracuda attack.

Nemo
He's a little fish with a big desire to see the world. Nemo was born with one weak fin, but nothing stops him from having fun.

Important Lesson
Marlin teaches Nemo everything—including how to brush himself on the fronds every day.

Marlin
Although he is a clownfish, Marlin is not really very funny. He only knows one joke!

Dad Knows Best
Nag, nag, nag! Sometimes Nemo feels like Marlin is always telling him what to do! Even the best of pals can fall out.

Dangerous Dare
Nemo is keen to prove to his dad that he is a brave fish. Once, as a dare, he swam off alone to touch a boat.

Dory Makes Three
Dory brings fun, friendship, and forgetfulness into the lives of this close clownfish family.

That's My Boy
Marlin has learnt to trust his son, and Nemo has discovered his stick-in-the-mud father is also kind of a hero.

SEA SCHOOL

Learning is fun when you have no classroom, no chalkboard, and no books! Mr. Ray's school is a daily journey of exploration, with plenty of singing. Dory loves helping out in class, where adventure is always on the timetable.

Sheldon
This playful seahorse has one tiny problem—he's H_2O intolerant! That's not great news for a fish who lives in the water!

Schoolyard
This sheltered spot with a soft, sandy bed is the perfect place for the young fish to play between lessons.

Tad
Tad is a butterfly fish who causes trouble to get attention. He is quite happy to admit that he is obnoxious.

Mr. Ray
Enthusiastic teacher Mr. Ray has enormous wings to carry his pupils on. With him in charge, lessons are never dull.

Wide-eyed Wonder
Riding on Mr. Ray's wing, with his classmates Sheldon and Pearl, Nemo is dazzled by the wonders of the deep.

Pearl
Friendly flapjack octopus Pearl has one tentacle shorter than the others. She doesn't like surprises as they make her squirt dark ink!

The Drop-off
Where the colorful coral reef ends, the ocean begins—the Drop-off can be a dangerous place for fish.

School of Thought
Mr. Ray has no classroom, but to him the sea is one big lesson of show and tell.

9

Use the extra stickers to create your own scene.

DORY'S SKILLS

She may lack a perfect memory, but this bubbly blue fish makes up for it with her wealth of hidden talents. Languages, letters, games, and guessing come naturally to her. She just loves getting involved in new challenges!

Memory Loss
Poor Dory forgets everything she has been told. How long has she had this problem? She can't remember.

Playing Games
Dory loves playing charades and gets a big kick out of the funny impressions of the playful moonfish.

Reading Human
Dory has a rare skill for a fish—she can read words. And if she keeps repeating them, she can remember them, too.

Talking Whale
Dory learned to speak whale when she was young, and regularly chatted to a whale shark. She is also fluent in humpback and in orca, too.

Sunny Side Up
Cheerful Dory can win anyone over with her positive outlook. "Just keep swimming" is her upbeat motto.

Hello Bruce!
Making friends comes naturally to Dory, who won't even run away from a shark. It could become a big new buddy!

Fearless Fish
Even in the darkest depths of the ocean an eerie glow seems like a friendly light to the trusting Dory.

Chirpy Tang
Dory is always sure things will turn out fine. Somehow, this forgetful fish is usually right!

Finding Friends
When Marlin is searching for Nemo, Dory helps him to find not just his son, but a new, blue friend for life.

LIFE AT THE MLI

Welcome to the Marine Life Institute, known as the Jewel of Morro Bay, California. Ocean creatures of every kind are brought here to recover from injury before being returned to the wild. Dory wants to stay—until she finds her long-lost family.

Fish out of Water
Marlin and Nemo watch helplessly as a staffer from the MLI lifts Dory out of the sea...

Slippery Customer?
Offbeat octopus Hank is keen to make a deal with Dory, take her transportation tag and leg it...

Bailey
A bump on the head affected this beluga whale's confidence. Now he thinks he's lost his power of echolocation.

Destiny
Best friend from Dory's childhood, this near-sighted whale shark has her own unique swimming style.

Hank
With so many limbs, maybe it's not surprising Hank can't resist offering a helping hand.

Becky
Becky is a wacky but sweet loon bird. She is easily distracted by spilled popcorn, but she's always there when Marlin calls "oo-roo!"

More Tangs
Oops! Marlin and Nemo get stuck in a tank of tangs, destined for Cleveland. Will Dory ever see her friends again?

Friends at the MLI
The whale exhibit is a seriously big attraction.

DANGERS OF THE DEEP

The big blue ocean can be a wonderful place, but for a little fish like Dory it can hold many perils. The sea is teeming with fascinating life—most of which is keen to eat you! Take a closer look, if you dare...

Anglerfish
This fiendish fisherman doesn't need to chase you —he'll lure you to him, with his friendly, glowing light.

Beastly Barracuda
Beware this most feared and deadly predator of the deep! A barracuda attacked Nemo's nest, and it was a miracle he survived.

Sea Snack
The sea is packed with eating machines. One false move and you're lunch!

Human Diver
He might mean well, but this collector of ailing fish may be a bit too keen to catch a special specimen for his aquarium.

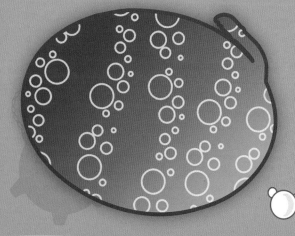

16

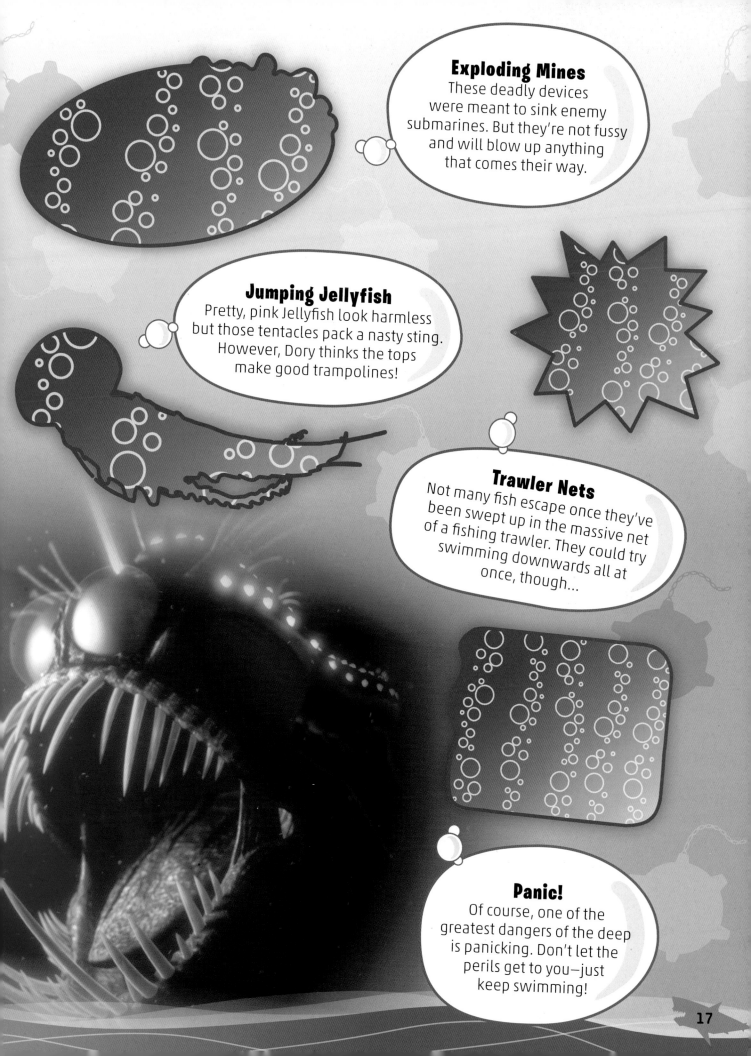

Exploding Mines
These deadly devices were meant to sink enemy submarines. But they're not fussy and will blow up anything that comes their way.

Jumping Jellyfish
Pretty, pink Jellyfish look harmless but those tentacles pack a nasty sting. However, Dory thinks the tops make good trampolines!

Trawler Nets
Not many fish escape once they've been swept up in the massive net of a fishing trawler. They could try swimming downwards all at once, though...

Panic!
Of course, one of the greatest dangers of the deep is panicking. Don't let the perils get to you—just keep swimming!

SWIMMING WITH SHARKS

Sharks have a scary reputation, but they are really much sweeter than they look—just ask Bruce and his gang. All they want is for everyone to take another look at sharks and see their cuddly, caring side.

Anchor
Anchor the hammerhead shark is very sensitive and doesn't like jokes about his looks. His wide-apart eyes give him extra-sharp vision.

Submarine
The cozy clubhouse of this well-meaning group is actually a sunken submarine, complete with live torpedoes.

Blenny
A new recruit to the group, this timid fish was invited along by Anchor. Attendance is far from relaxing for nervous Blenny.

Bruce

The friendliest great white shark you could ever meet, Bruce is changing the image of sharks with his campaign: Fish are friends, not food!

Vegetarian Meeting

Bruce's meetings encourage fish to give up their bad habit of eating each other. The members tell their stories and share veggie snacks.

Chum

This toothy mako shark loves all sea life—except dolphins. They always show off about how cute they are.

Toothy Grins

Don't judge these sharks by the look of their seriously scary teeth—they are no monsters.

Lending a Fin

The shark gang never forgets its friends and loves to visit the reef to see if Dory and her pals need any help or advice.

FISH FRIENDSHIP

An unfunny clownfish and a cheerful Regal Tang—they have little in common, yet somehow they make a great team. Both have a talent for getting in—and out of—trouble. And both will admit they have grown to become true friends.

First Meeting
Not all friendships get off to the perfect start. When Marlin first met Dory she offered to help him—then wondered why Marlin was following her!

Ditzy Dory
At first Marlin didn't trust Dory's advice. He soon changed his mind when she helped him escape from inside a whale!

Telling Tales
Dory makes a great companion, as Marlin can tell her the same joke over and over again.

Saving Dory
Marlin risks a hundred stings to rescue Dory from the jellyfish. He regrets not listening to her advice about which way to swim.

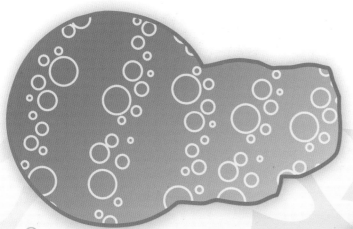

Sticking Together
Good friends stay together whatever happens. At least when things go wrong, they'll always have someone else to blame!

Teamwork
Two heads are better than one. Dory and Marlin work together to solve their problems, like when they both escape with the diver's mask.

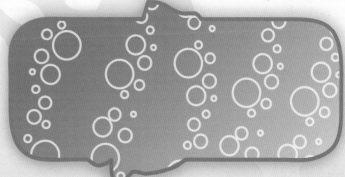

Combining Skills
Both friends bring different skills to their partnership. While Dory reads the writing on the mask, Marlin distracts the mad anglerfish!

Ups and Downs
Even best friends have bad days. Marlin once thought he should leave Dory behind, but he soon realized how much he would miss her.

21

THE QUEST FOR DORY

Marlin and Nemo are so fond of Dory that they will face any danger to get her back again. Along the way they meet an assortment of amazing creatures who are only too happy to help them on their perilous quest.

Feathered Friend
This likable loon bird is a friend of the sea lions. She will always help out, especially if they are polite and call her "Rebecca darling."

Adorable Otter
Always making a splash, the playful otter is one of the special sights tourists love to see in the bay.

Otter Party
One otter is cute but a whole romp of otters is sweet enough to stop traffic—which happens quite regularly.

Sea Lions
Lazing on the rocks is living the dream for these guys. Rudder and Fluke just love "lion" around!

Gerald
Jolly Gerald is happy to lend out his bucket, as long as he gets his reward—a chance to sit on Rudder and Fluke's favorite rock!

Loon Lift
Ooo-roo! Becky agrees to give Marlin and Nemo a lift into the MLI, although Marlin is wondering if perhaps they should have tried another airline.

Reunited
It's amazing who you can bump into in the pipe system of the MLI— three friends have a happy reunion.

OCEAN ENCOUNTERS

You're never alone in the ocean—there's always someone ready to offer a helping fin to a fish in trouble. Whether it's totally radical turtles or a well-meaning whale, an act of kindness can come at any time, from any place.

Crush

150 years young, this cool dude will help anyone in need. He knows how to surf life's gnarly waves and just go with the flow.

The EAC

To make speed across the sea, jump aboard the EAC—the East Australian Current. The turtles use it as a high-speed highway.

Turtle Friends

Sharing stories with those you meet is a great way to make friends. Forgetful Dory can enjoy the same story over and over again!

Squirt

Crush's son is learning how to stand on his own four flippers and tackle the crazy currents of the Coral Sea alone.

The Whale
The blue whale is the largest living creature in the world. He may seem scary, but in fact has a gentle nature.

Pointing the Way
You'll never get lost with moonfish around—these guys will impersonate a road sign to help strangers in need.

Moorish Mystery
This mysterious, Moorish idol fish is full of crazy plans. But Nemo finds out that Gill can also be a trustworthy friend.

Turtle-y Awesome
Riding the currents, the helpful turtles are friendly guides through the ocean.

IN THE TANK

Not all fish live out on the reef like Dory and her pals. Nemo has friends in a state-of-the-art aquarium in Wallaby Way, Sydney. Meet some of the pampered pets whose water is always pure and perfectly filtered.

Gill
A rebel at heart. This Moorish idol fish believes fish were never meant to live in a box.

Peach
This starfish is an eagle-eyed look-out girl. She loves to spy on the world outside the tank.

Jacques
No-one gets scummy in the tank with this super-fussy cleaner shrimp on the case.

Bubbles
Bubbles is called Bubbles because he loves bubbles! They pop out of his personal treasure chest.

Bloat
Easily upset, Bloat balloons to giant size when excited. He hates it when the others play volleyball with him.

Use the extra stickers to create your own scene.

LIFE ON THE SURFACE

Adventurous fish like Dory meet creatures above the waves as well as below. Sydney Harbour has visitors of the feathered, finny, and crabby kind. They'll always share a yarn with you—if they're not trying to gobble you up!

Pelican Alert
Little fish have to beware in the big city. Dory spots a pelican who sees reef-fish as an exotic snack!

Seagulls
These scavengers are the greediest gulls around. Their catch phrase is: "Mine!" because they think everything edible belongs to them.

Nigel the Pelican
Not all seabirds spend their lives trying to eat fish. Nigel just loves to chat with them, especially the guys in the dentist's tank.

Bernie the Crab
This local loves snacking on the treats that leak from the city's outlet pipe. Bernie knows all the harbor gossip.

Gull Getaway
If there's one thing a pelican loves it's being faster than the local seagulls. Nigel helps Dory and Marlin escape from them.

Dentist Chaos
They may think they own the planet, but humans are not so smart. They can be very quick to panic when their pets escape!

Sydney Harbour
Don't be fooled—this peaceful-looking spot contains a world of life.

ESCAPE!

Under the sea there are countless ways to get into trouble—and even more ways to get out of it! The key is inventing an unexpected way out of a crisis. Luckily, Dory and her friends are loaded with imagination.

Masked Menace
The anglerfish is a clever hunter, but it doesn't have the brains to get out of a diving mask once it's stuck.

A Whale of a Time
Stuck in a whale, Dory uses her language skills to discuss an exit strategy. Riding the water spout is a fun trip.

Jelly Jump
Surrounded by jellyfish, Marlin invents a game of bouncing on the tops. It's their only chance of escaping alive!

Top Tactics
Gill taught Nemo to swim down when caught in a net. Nemo passes this on to all the fish caught by the trawler.

Nemo the Hero
Gill teaches Nemo to believe in himself. Only then can he break the filter system and launch their escape plan.

Pay Attention
Reading is an important skill—especially when you're reading a sign that says "escape."

Stubborn Streak
Marlin is stubborn and refuses to be swallowed by Gerald the pelican. The bird never had so much trouble with his grub!

Think Ahead
When planning an escape you should work out every detail. How did you plan to get out of the bags, Gill?

WHAT WOULD DORY DO?

She doesn't realize it, but with her smiles, songs, and crazy ideas, Dory is a big source of inspiration to others. And with the habit they all have of getting into trouble, they need all the inspiration they can get!

Leap of Faith
It's one giant leap for fishkind. Dory knows when to make a quick exit and that all drains lead to the sea...

Awesome Allies
You need friends to help you along the way, and Dory finds awesome allies, like Hank, wherever she goes.

Fountain Flyers
Dory's daring attitude is catching. How else would Nemo get the idea of riding a water fountain?

Memory Power
Memories of her childhood home don't make Dory sad—they just make her even more determined to get back there again.

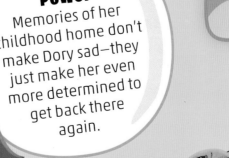

Coral Corner

Sea View

Sponge Beds

Handsome Hutch

Crossing Guard

Dangerous Dare

Nemo

Sole Survivor

Dad Knows Best

Marlin

Spanish Dancer

Dory Makes Three

That's My Boy

Best of Fronds

Mr. Ray

Sheldon

Tad

The Drop-off

Schoolyard

Pearl

Wide-eyed
Wonder

© Disney/Pixar

Playing Games

© Disney/Pixar

© Disney/Pixar

Fearless Fish

© Disney/Pixar

© Disney/Pixar

© Disney/Pixar

© Disney/Pixar

P. SHERMAN
42 WALLABY WAY
SYDNEY, NSW

Reading Human

© Disney/Pixar

© Disney/Pixar

© Disney/Pixar

Hello Bruce!

© Disney/Pixar

© Disney/Pixar

© Disney/Pixar

© Disney/Pixar

Memory Loss

© Disney/Pixar

Talking Whale

© Disney/Pixar

© Disney/Pixar

© Disney/Pixar

© Disney/Pixar

© Disney/Pixar

Finding Friends

Sunny Side Up

© Disney/Pixar

© Disney/Pixar

Beastly Barracuda

© Disney/Pixar

Human Diver

© Disney/Pixar

Anglerfish

© Disney/Pixar

Trawler Nets

© Disney/Pixar

Jumping Jellyfish

© Disney/Pixar

Exploding Mines

© Disney/Pixar

Panic!

© Disney/Pixar

Submarine

Lending a Fin

© Disney/Pixar

© Disney/Pixar

© Disney/Pixar

© Disney/Pixar

© Disney/Pixar

© Disney/Pixar

© Disney/Pixar

Bruce

© Disney/Pixar

© Disney/Pixar

Vegetarian Meeting

© Disney/Pixar

© Disney/Pixar

© Disney/Pixar

© Disney/Pixar

© Disney/Pixar

© Disney/Pixar

Blenny

© Disney/Pixar

© Disney/Pixar

© Disney/Pixar

© Disney/Pixar

© Disney/Pixar

Anchor

© Disney/Pixar

© Disney/Pixar

Chum

© Disney/Pixar

Saving Dory

First Meeting

Teamwork

Ups and Downs

Sticking Together

Ditzy Dory

Combining Skills

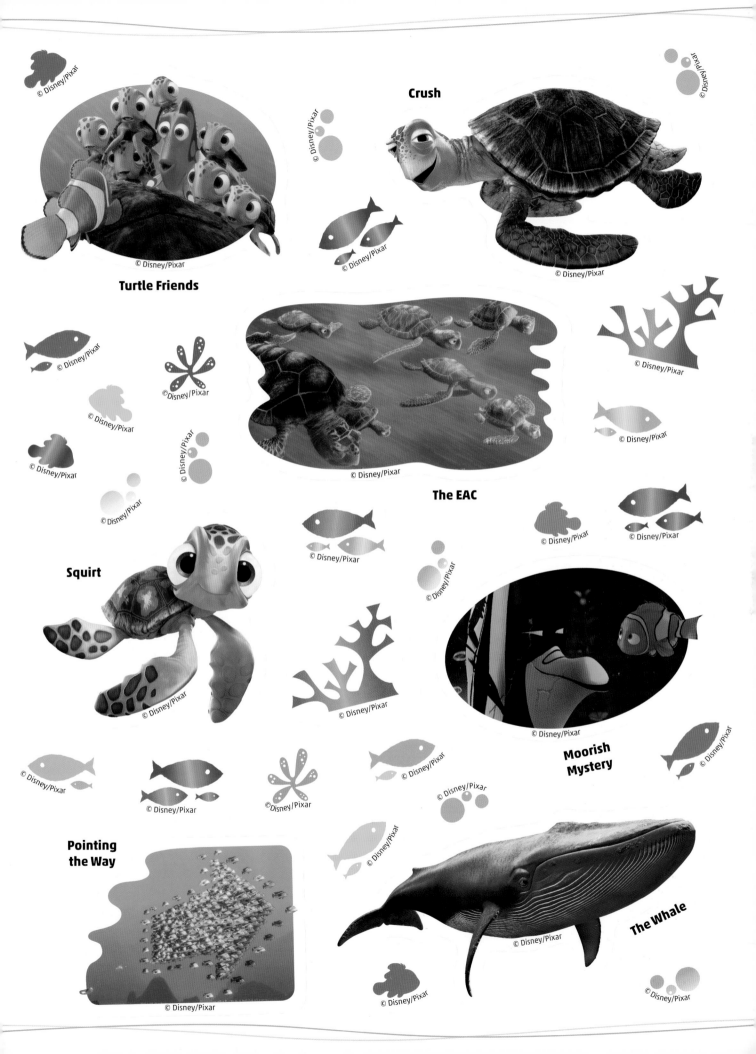

Crush

Turtle Friends

The EAC

Squirt

Moorish Mystery

Pointing the Way

The Whale

© Disney/Pixar

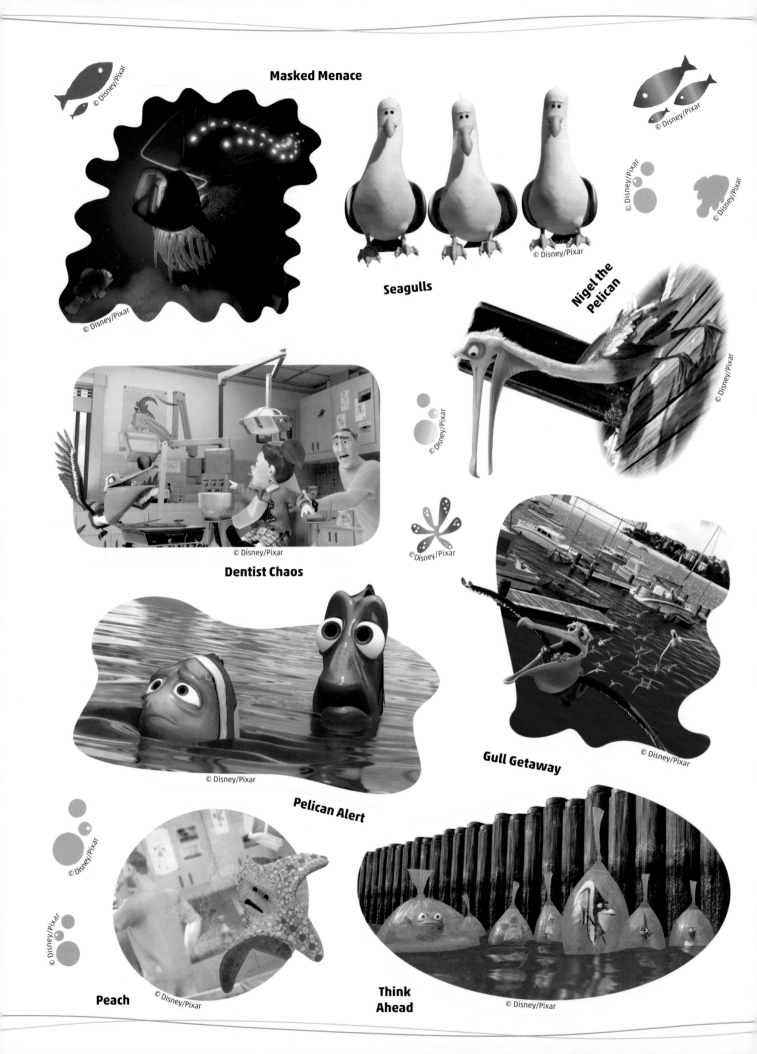

Masked Menace

Seagulls

Nigel the Pelican

Dentist Chaos

Gull Getaway

Pelican Alert

Peach

Think Ahead

Bernie the Crab

© Disney/Pixar

© Disney/Pixar

Bubbles

© Disney/Pixar

© Disney/Pixar

© Disney/Pixar

© Disney/Pixar

Top Tactics

© Disney/Pixar

Jelly Jump

© Disney/Pixar

© Disney/Pixar

A Whale of a Time

© Disney/Pixar

© Disney/Pixar

Jacques

Nemo the Hero

© Disney/Pixar

© Disney/Pixar

© Disney/Pixar

© Disney/Pixar

Gill

© Disney/Pixar

Bloat

© Disney/Pixar

Stubborn Streak

Baby Dory

A New Life

Lost!

Meeting Marlin

Mama Dory

Remembering

Dory's Dad

Bailey

© Disney/Pixar

Becky

Hank

Fish out of Water

More Tangs

Slippery Customer?

Adorable Otter

Destiny

Otter Party

Loon Lift

Feathered Friend

Sea Lions

Gerald

Fountain Flyers

Awesome Allies

Memory Power

Leap of Faith

Extra Stickers

Extra Stickers

Extra Stickers

Extra Stickers

Extra Stickers

© Disney/Pixar

Extra Stickers

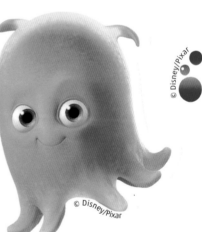

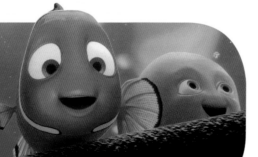

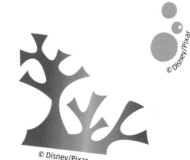

Extra Stickers

© Disney/Pixar

© Disney/Pixar

© Disney/Pixar

© Disney/Pixar

© Disney/Pixar

© Disney/Pixar

© Disney/Pixar

© Disney/Pixar

P. SHERMAN
42 WALLABY WAY
SYDNEY, NSW

© Disney/Pixar

© Disney/Pixar

© Disney/Pixar

© Disney/Pixar

© Disney/Pixar

© Disney/Pixar

© Disney/Pixar

© Disney/Pixar

© Disney/Pixar

© Disney/Pixar

© Disney/Pixar

© Disney/Pixar

© Disney/Pixar

© Disney/Pixar

Extra Stickers

© Disney/Pixar

Extra Stickers

© Disney/Pixar

Extra Stickers

© Disney/Pixar

Extra Stickers

Extra Stickers

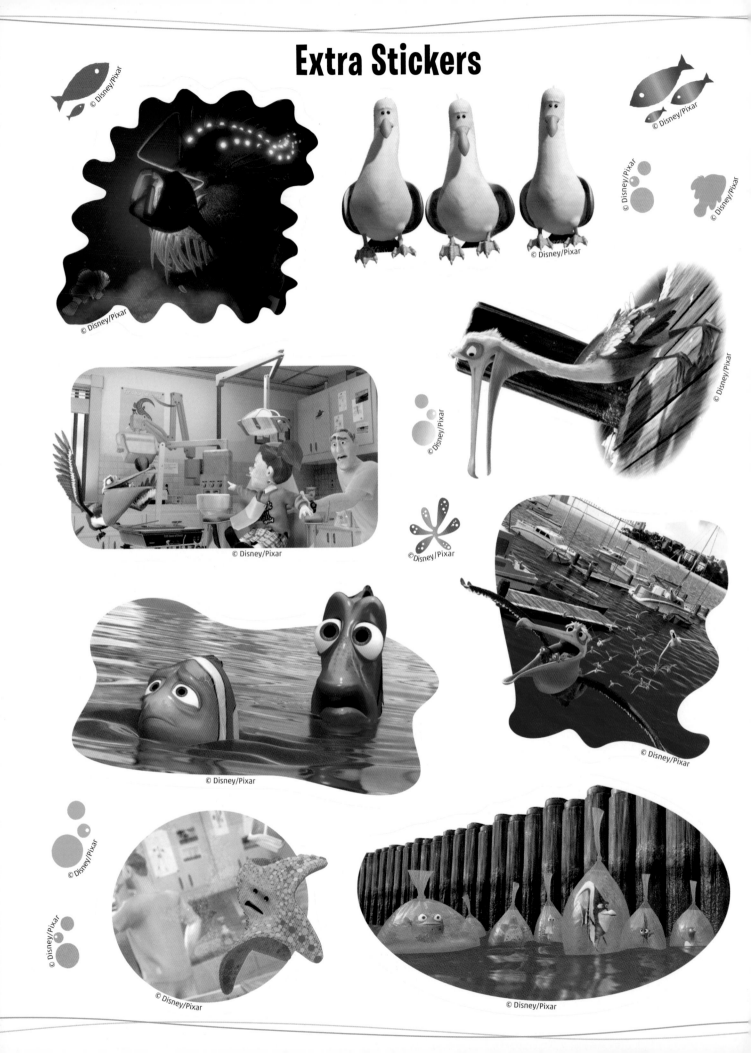

© Disney/Pixar

Extra Stickers

Extra Stickers

© Disney/Pixar

Extra Stickers

Extra Stickers

Extra Stickers